Diary of a Horse Mad Girl

Book 1

My First Pony

By Katrina Kahler

D1508648

Dedication

This book is dedicated to my beautiful daughter. These are her adventures and we all loved going along for the ride. I hope you do too!

Hi, my name is Abbie and this diary is all about me and my very first pony, Sparkle who is a beautiful 13 hand Palomino. She is the best first pony anyone could wish for and we've had so many great adventures together. Luckily, I live on a rural property with lots of land and also other neighborhood girls to ride with. We have our very own "Saddle Club" and it's such a great way to grow up. I have many fun times to share with you and if you're anywhere near as horse mad as me, I'm sure you'll enjoy reading this book.

Now, from the beginning…

Monday 24 September

When I heard Sparkle nicker this morning, I knew she was calling me. I raced over to the paddock still in my PJs. I couldn't get there quickly enough! I can't believe I now actually have my own pony! And she's such a beautiful palomino. They've always been my favorite type of horse and now I have one of my very own. It's like a dream come true. One minute, I'm being led around the paddock on my neighbor's horse and the next minute I'm standing there with my own palomino.

I'm lucky as well, to have a girl like Ali as my neighbor. She's really nice to me and also a great rider. If it wasn't for her living next door with horses of her own, this probably wouldn't be happening. She and her mum know everything there is to know about horses, which is such a great help, because my parents don't know much at all. And now that I have my own pony to ride, we can go riding together. It's great having an older girl next door who is as horse mad as me. I always wanted a big sister. I'm very lucky!

And guess what! Sparkle loves bananas. Who would ever have thought that horses would eat bananas – with the skin and all! I'm going to give her one every day as a special treat. I'll have to make sure Mom buys lots of carrots as well. I'm so glad it's the school holidays and I can spend every day with her. My new grooming kit is really cool too – it's in a special pink box and everything in it is pink. And the best part is…Sparkle loves being brushed. She's such a good pony and Ali says I'm very lucky to have found a pony with a quiet temperament like hers.

I can't wait for my first riding lesson on Thursday. The instructor is coming at 9:00 in the morning before it gets hot, so I'll have to be up early to make sure I'm ready. I don't think I'll be able to sleep tonight, just thinking about it! I'm so excited!!!

Thursday 27 September

I thought that the day Sparkle arrived at our place was the best day of my life, but I think today was even better. That riding lesson was so awesome and Jane, the instructor, says I'm a natural. She said I have a really good seat and Mom was commenting on my posture and how straight I sit in the saddle. I just have to work on pulling Sparkle up when I want her to slow down. Even though she's 16 years old, she's very forward moving. But that's why she's such a good sporting pony and I can't wait to see Josh ride her in the gymkhana on Sunday.

He was really sad to sell her, but she's too small for him now. His new horse Tara, is beautiful, but Josh says that Sparkle is the best sporting pony and he's really keen to do well in the gymkhana. Anyway, I agreed to let him take her this Sunday so he can compete on her one last time. I can't wait to go and watch! I've never been to a gymkhana before; it's going to be so much fun.

And Ali said that we could go riding together tomorrow. That will be cool. She'll be able to give me a lesson and help me improve my riding. Mom said I can only ride in the small paddock though, until Sparkle and I get used to each other.

Ali and I are becoming really close; I think she's my best friend now. And it's fun sitting in our special tree. That's what we've decided to do now when we finish riding each day - take some snacks, climb up and sit in our special tree in the big paddock and just watch the horses grazing. Mom says I now have my very own saddle club. That's my favorite TV show but I never thought I'd have a saddle club of my own. IT'S TOTALLY COOL!

Sunday 29 September

Oh my gosh, today was AMAZING!!! Sparkle won 4 blue ribbons, 2 red and one green and Josh gave them all to me. I'm so happy!

Sparkle is the best sporting pony, I can't wait to do gymkhanas on her myself. That bounce pony looks like so much fun and Sparkle is really good at it. And she's so good at barrels as well. But the jumping was the best – Sparkle is such a good all-rounder! Of course, Josh is a really good rider and really pushed her on, but I know I'll be able to do that too. Especially on Sparkle. What a talented pony!

And she looked so pretty today. I spent all yesterday afternoon getting her ready. It was so much fun in the paddock with Ali. We bathed her with this special horsey shampoo that made her coat look really shiny and Ali showed me how to braid her mane and tail as well. It looked very professional, especially with the colored ribbon that we braided through it. And the brow band that Josh's Mom made for her looked terrific. She said that I can keep it and she's even going to make me another one with ribbon the colors of my pony club, when I eventually join.

I can't wait till school goes back and I can tell all my friends about her – they'll be so jealous! I wonder if I'd be able to take her to school for show and tell? Miss Johnson might let me!

Tuesday 2 October

I can't believe it! Cammie and Grace now have a horse too. They're the girls who moved in across the road recently and with all 4 of us, we can have a proper saddle club. Four girls in the one street all with horses. They have to share Rocket – that's the name of their new horse (apparently he's really fast).

We're planning to meet up in the big paddock tomorrow. They don't have anywhere to keep Rocket but Ali's mum said it's fine for him to stay in their paddock for the time being. We'll all be able to go riding together. Their dad knows heaps about horses as well. He grew up on a horse property, so I guess he'll teach them how to ride.

I'm having another riding lesson with Jane tomorrow. This time I'm going to work on my rising trot. Ali's been teaching me how to do it properly already, so I bet Jane will be surprised at how good I am.

Sparkle loves the new hay that we've bought – it's top quality grass hay and as soon as she sees me with it, she comes cantering over. She's such a beautiful pony, the other girls all think so as well. I'm so lucky to have a palomino – she's definitely the prettiest horse!

Friday 5 October

IT'S NOT FAIR! Ali is MY friend and the tree in the big paddock is OUR special tree! Now Cammie has come along and taken Ali off me. They spent the whole afternoon together in the paddock with the horses and Ali showed Cammie our tree. That's where I found them when I finally got home today after going to the saddlery with Mom. She bought me a brand new pink feed bucket that is really cool. I was so happy because I found lots of things that I'd like for my birthday as well. It's only a month away and Mom said that she'd think about them. Hopefully she'll go back and buy them for me. Anyway, I raced over to the paddock to show Sparkle and give her a banana and there they were…both Ali and Cammie up in our tree together. And the worst part was that they weren't even interested in me. It's probably because they're the same age and I'm younger but it's not fair – Ali is MY special friend!

Mom said that we'll all have to just get along and that I can spend time with Grace, who is more my age. But I'm really upset about Ali. I can see that she and Cammie are going to become best friends now. I liked it when it was just the two of us. Why did the other girls have to come along and spoil it all?

Sunday 7 October

It was really scary today! My friend Ella came over with her brother Tim just as I was getting ready to go for a ride. Anyway, Mom said they could come to the paddock with us to have a little ride themselves. They were so excited as neither of them had ever been on a horse before.

Mom put the saddle on while I did up the bridle (Mom still can't figure out how to put it on properly). We led Ella around the paddock first. She was having such a great time. Then Tim decided that he wanted a turn. To make it a bit more exciting, Mom got Sparkle to trot while she was leading her. But then all of a sudden she turned Sparkle to the left. It was a really sharp turn. Sparkle was fine but it made the saddle slip completely down to her side. She just kept trotting along, not worried in the slightest, but Tim was almost on the ground.

Mom hadn't done the girth up tightly enough! She should know by now that it gets loose after a few minutes of riding. We all thought it looked so funny with Tim hanging on like that. Sparkle wasn't going very fast and he was hanging on really tightly so he was actually okay. But he didn't think so! It scared him half to death. He was even shaking. I'd forgotten it was his first ride on a horse – EVER – and he just isn't used to it. I hope this doesn't put him off riding.

But it was what happened next that scared EVERYBODY! Someone must have left the gate open because Rocket had wandered into Sparkle's paddock. When he saw us all gathered around Tim and Sparkle, he got all stirred up and galloped over. All of a sudden, he did a huge kick and came SO close to kicking Ella in the head. His hooves looked like they just missed her!

She screamed and this made him go even crazier. I think it

was the scariest thing I've ever seen! Just before that, all of us were laughing at Tim. Watching him slide down Sparkle's side while she trotted along looked pretty funny. But then in the blink of an eye Ella was almost being kicked in the head by a huge horse. Mom was still freaking out about it after dinner tonight – she said she can't stop thinking about what could have happened. I don't think she'll ever forget to tighten the girth again, that's for sure!

Actually, I don't think any of us will ever forget what happened today!

And now I have to go back to school tomorrow. At least I can see all my friends and tell them about Sparkle. (I don't want to tell them about the near accident though – they mightn't want to come over if I do).

As soon as I get home, I'm going to race over to the paddock and give Sparkle a banana. I hope we have some. I'd better go and check – if there's none maybe Mom can get some more on her way home from work.

Monday 8 October

School was so boring today. I just wanted to come home to Sparkle. All I could think about was my baby. I told all my friends about her and they're so jealous! They all wish that they had a horse. Everyone wants to come over and have a ride. Mom said, maybe not just yet. She's still getting over what happened yesterday. At least Ella is okay – and Tim as well. Ella and I were laughing about what happened to him. That was the funniest thing. But he doesn't think so.

Sparkle loved her banana this afternoon. I didn't ride, I just patted her and watched her grazing. She's the prettiest horse! I could see Ali and Cammie with their horses over at Ali's place. They waved to me but didn't come over.

I knew they'd become best friends. I don't know where Grace was.

At least I have my baby – Sparkle...AND my darling cat Soxy – I know that THEY love me!!!!

Wednesday 10 October

Dad put an ad in the paper to see if we can agist our big paddock. If we can get someone to keep their horse here, the money will help to pay for Sparkle's feed and my riding lessons. And just tonight a lady rang. She's coming over tomorrow to have a look. Dad said that she has a daughter who needs somewhere to keep her horse. She has a friend with another 2 horses as well and she doesn't have anywhere to keep them either. The lady told Dad that the girls are both good riders. They're about 4 years older than me but he said she sounded very nice and he thinks this could work out really well. Maybe the girls will be able to help me with my riding? Maybe we'll even become good friends! That would be cool, especially now that Ali is spending all her time with Cammie and Grace. It will be so good to have some other horsey friends of my own.

I hope they're friendly and that they do decide to keep their horses here. I can't wait to meet them tomorrow. I wonder what their horses are like? I hope they get along with Sparkle!

Thursday 11 October

Shelley and Kate are super nice and their horses are gorgeous. They love our place and think it'll be perfect. This is going to be so cool. If I introduce them to Cammie, Grace and Ali, they might even be happy to include me again and that means we can have a real saddle club – there'll be so many of us. I just wish we had proper stables like in the Saddle Club TV show. That would be really cool. But instead, we have to cross over our creek to get to the horse paddocks and it's so far to walk, especially carrying all the tack. I'm glad Mom carries the saddle for me!

Shelley and Kate are going to bring their horses to our place on Saturday and we've planned to go riding together. This is so exciting, I can't wait! And they've even said that they'll pay me to feed their horses each day. That's so good because now I'll be able to save up and buy those really pretty jodhpurs that I saw at Saddle World last weekend. Mom said I'm going to have to get up even earlier in the mornings now, so that I'm ready for school on time. But I don't mind.

Saturday 13 October

Our place is just like the Saddle Club now! Shelley and Kate brought their horses over today and we all went riding together. Then we spent the afternoon bathing and grooming them. It's so much fun having girls at my house and doing all this horsey stuff together. It's way better than having to do it on my own. Mom says the problem with Cammie and Grace is that they're keeping their horses at Ali's and that's why they've become best friends. But I have my own special horsey friends now. And they're keeping their horses at my house.

This afternoon we all just got to hang out and talk about horses. Shelley has a bay and Kate has a chestnut. The other horse is a paint and he belongs to Kate as well, but she doesn't ride him much. Sparkle seems to get along with them all so that's really good. And now she has lots of horses in the paddocks around hers so she definitely won't get lonely.

We met Kate's dad today when he brought the horses over and he told us that we could borrow his horse trailer anytime. This means I might be able to go to pony club when it starts up again next year. Shelley and Kate have told me all about it and it sounds amazing! I can't wait for that!

Sunday 14 October

A sound like thunder woke me up at 5:30 this morning. At first I couldn't work out what it was because I was still half asleep. But then I realized it was horses' hooves galloping past my bedroom window. I heard Mom and Dad running down the stairs so I jumped out of bed and ran up the driveway after them.

Shelley and Kate's horses had escaped from the paddock and ran down the hill and across the creek. There's not much water in it at the moment and it's easy to cross. They must have been trying to get out the front gate but luckily they found the big feed bins that we keep in the shed. At least that stopped them from going out onto the road! We found them up there stuffing themselves with whatever they could find. Luckily it was only chaff but Mom and Dad were in a panic. The horses were really excited and stirring each other up, especially Nugget. He's the paint and he seemed to be the ringleader.

Mom, Dad and I were all running around in our PJs, with lead ropes and some hay, trying to catch them all. Mom and Dad were NOT impressed - especially at 5:30 in the morning! It was so hard to catch them and calm them down. Luckily there were 3 of us – It took quite a while to get them under control and back in their paddock. Dad then had to fix the gate.

What a way to start the day!

Dad rang Tom (Kate's dad) and he said that Nugget is an escape artist. When Shelley and Kate came over this afternoon, they said that he's escaped from a lot of paddocks. Dad was annoyed because Tom hadn't told us that before. He's going to try to find somewhere else to keep Nugget now. This will be good because we don't want that happening again!

At least we all got to go for a ride. When we went over to the paddock, Ali, Cammie and Grace were riding at Ali's. Our paddock is the best one for riding in though because it's so big. I introduced them to Shelley and Kate and asked them if they wanted to ride with us. Ali, Cammie and Grace were SO nice to me. I could see that they really wanted to be friends with the older girls as well. But Cammie's probably a bit jealous – I know that she wants to keep Ali to herself.

It was heaps of fun with us all riding together though and hopefully now we can all meet up after school one day this week and go riding again – that will be awesome if we do!

I hope the girls get on okay. It'd be great if we can all become good friends!

Kate's paint - Nugget

The Escape Artitst!!!

Monday 15 October

When I got home from school today, I found that Nugget was missing from the paddock. I was so worried because I thought he'd escaped again but then Dad told me they've found somewhere else to keep him. Dad was really relieved and said it would be less to worry about. It's also one less horse for me to have to feed each morning and night. But that means less money as well and that's not good because I really want to be able to buy those jodhpurs as soon as I can.

I'm really excited though because Tom, Kate's Dad, brought a heap of horse jumps over and put them in the paddock. Kate's horse Lulu is a really good jumper and Kate loves jumping so she wants to practice. Tom said that he'd teach me how to jump on Sparkle as well. This is very exciting – I really want to learn how to jump – it looks like so much fun. It'll probably be scary at first but Tom said I can just go over little jumps until I become confident. I know that Sparkle is a good jumper as well, so I'm sure she'll love it too. This is so cool!!!

Wednesday 17 October

I had a great time this afternoon. There were actually all 6 of us riding in the paddock together and everyone was so friendly to each other. I was really worried about that, especially with Cammie and I didn't know how it would work out. But even though we're all different ages, we get on really well. Shelley is the oldest – she's 13, Kate and Ali are both 12, Cammie is 11 and Grace and I are both 9. (Well, I'll turn 9 in just over three weeks' time – and I can't wait)!

And I got to try jumping!!! Kate and Shelley were telling me what to do. They were only small jumps but I loved it and so did Sparkle. Her ears went forward and she didn't even hesitate. I love her so much!

I saw a beautiful Wintec saddle at the saddlery on the weekend as well and I really hope that Mom and Dad buy it for my birthday present. It'll be so much easier to jump in than the Western saddle I'm using now. Ali's mom said I could borrow that until I get my own saddle. It's a great one to learn in because it helps hold me in place and I have less chance of falling off. But it's hard to rise up properly when I go for a jump.

The new Wintecs are so pretty and Shelley has one. She says it's fantastic. I'd really like to get some chaps of my own as well. Ali has loaned me her old pair but she has new ones and they look so cool. I should have enough money soon, but I want to get those jodhpurs as well – there are so many things I want to buy. Maybe I should just put them on my Christmas list?

I wonder if I'll get a new saddle for my birthday? I hope so! I can't wait!!!

Saturday 20 October

Mom was the only one at home today but it was lucky that she was there. Kate was trotting Lulu down the hill so she could hose her down after riding but her hoof got caught in some wire fencing. It's part of a gate that Dad made and someone left it lying across the track. Kate said that Lulu panicked and got all tangled up in it. Kate fell off her and it was so lucky that she wasn't hurt but Lulu's legs were all cut to pieces.

Shelley ran down to the house to get Mom and they managed to untangle Lulu. But her legs were really badly cut and Mom had to call the vet. Thank goodness Lulu's going to be okay! Kate's not going to be able to ride her until she heals though and that could take a couple of weeks! Kate was really upset and rang her Dad. She said he got really angry and wants to talk to us about paying the vet bill.

Now Mom and Dad are upset – they don't want to have to pay someone else's vet bill! I don't know what's going to happen. I hope that the girls can still stay here. It's been so much better since they arrived - the others are so much nicer to me now and we're all able to ride together. It has to work out.

Monday 22 October

We had visitors this afternoon and they left the front gate open! I'd brought Sparkle down to graze on the nice grass around the house and when I went to check on her, I couldn't find her anywhere. I just knew that she'd probably walked up the driveway and out the gate.

Mom and I raced down the street looking for her. We were so worried that she might have wandered down towards the main road. We couldn't see her anywhere so we headed up to the horsey property at the end of our street in case she'd gone there but no one had seen her.

We had to look down every driveway and Mom was getting really stressed. Then we walked up Cammie and Grace's driveway and that was like climbing a mountain, it's so steep. It was the only place we hadn't been to though. Then all of a sudden we spotted her in amongst some bushes. But as soon as she saw us, she decided to bolt. I didn't think we were going to be able to catch her at all but luckily I took a banana with me. She just couldn't resist! Then we managed to get the halter and lead rope on her and walk her home.

I'm so glad we found her – I don't know what I would have done if she'd gone missing! We're going to have to put a sign on the gate so people close it when they come in, in future.

Mom and Dad can't believe so many things have gone wrong since Sparkle arrived. At least it's all sorted out with Kate's dad now. He came over and worked out the vet bill with Dad. He's blaming us for the wire gate that was lying across the track. We don't know whose fault that was but Dad's just going to give him free agistment for a couple of weeks. Anyway, he's happy with that. And thank goodness Lulu is going to be okay. She just has to rest for another 10 days or so and then Kate should be able to ride her again. I'm so pleased about that and so is Kate. It would be terrible to have a horse and not be able to ride her!

My baby. I'm so glad she's safe!!!

Wednesday 7 November

I just haven't had a chance to write lately – I've been so busy looking after all the horses - especially now that the girls want me to rug them. This keeps their coats looking nice and stops them from getting bitten. I really need to get a summer rug for Sparkle as well. It's so much extra work putting the rugs on and off, but at least the summer ones can stay on all day. They actually protect the horses and help to keep them cool. I didn't know that! I'll definitely have to get one for my baby!

I'm SO excited because this Sunday is my birthday!!! – Finally! And all my friends are coming over for a pool party sleepover on Saturday. I can't wait to show them Sparkle. Mom said that we'll be able to give them pony rides on the grass by the pool. She said that she'll put Sparkle on a lead rope and lead them around. I can't wait!

I wonder if I'll get that new saddle? Mom and Dad said they won't tell me what they've got for me. They said it's a surprise and I have to wait. I hope it's the Wintec! I'm so excited – I'm definitely not going to be able to sleep tonight.

Sunday 11 November

It was the BEST BIRTHDAY EVER!!!!!

My party was amazing! Everyone arrived yesterday afternoon and the first thing they wanted to do was see Sparkle – they think she's so pretty and they all wanted to pat and brush her. I think she loved the attention. They all loved riding her as well. Mom and I led them around on the lead rope. Of course we made sure that the girth was extra tight and everyone was safe. Most of them live in suburban houses and don't get to be on a property so they always enjoy coming to my house. It's so much better now that I have a horse though!

And Nate even gave them rides on his motorbike. He can be the best brother when he wants to be! I think he was proud to show off his new bike and was more than happy to give all my friends a double around our house. That's another great thing about Sparkle, she's totally bomb proof and doesn't get scared of anything really. Her last owner Josh, rode motorbikes too, so I guess she's become used to them. This is great because it doesn't bother her at all when Nate and his friends ride their bikes in the paddock near hers.

My party ended up being heaps of fun – we spent hours in the pool, jumping off our diving deck. It's the best thing and we were all lining up in a row, holding hands and jumping in together. Mom took some great action photos as well with us in mid-air – they're so cool! The trampoline by the pool is heaps of fun as well and everyone just loved it. Dad set up lights around the pool area and also a mirror ball in the gazebo with lots of black plastic for the lights to shine on. We had flame torches lit in the garden as well and it was so beautiful once it got dark. Everyone was commenting on how pretty it looked.

After dinner, we had a disco in the gazebo and the mirror ball and all the lights looked awesome. Everyone thinks I'm so lucky that my dad is a musician because he set up his big speakers for us and even some microphones with stands for us to sing. We had the music really loud and everyone was dancing and singing and having so much fun. We played really cool games as well like Freeze, where you have to stand still when the music stops and also the limbo.

Mom and Dad had set up our big family tent down on the grass and we all slept in there. What a great night – a bit squashy but we all managed to fit. Ali, Cammie, Grace and I talked about horsey stuff all night. We hardly got any sleep. I'm so glad they came – we're getting on really well now and Grace and I are becoming great friends. It's probably because we're more the same age. Everyone else was telling us to be quiet because they wanted to go to sleep. I guess we all eventually drifted off, but I'm sure it was really late when we did.

Then today, we spent pretty much the whole day in the pool – and singing on the microphones as well. Tina, my best friend from school wouldn't stop. Dad said that you could hear her all the way down our driveway and we're sure our neighbors were glad when she finally went home. I think she wants to be a rock star when she gets older. Hopefully her voice improves!

And then late this afternoon after everyone left, Mom and Dad gave me my present. And it's the WINTEC!! They wanted to wait until everyone had gone so we could have some special family time together. Oh my gosh, I was so excited when I saw what it was. It looks so shiny and new – especially after riding the old western style saddle that Ali's Mom has been lending me. I was so used to that.

I'm really going to look after my new saddle. It comes in a

special protective bag that I can keep it in when I'm not riding. Mom said that Sparkle and I won't know ourselves – I'm sure that she's going to find it much more comfortable as well.

I can't wait to go riding tomorrow and show the girls. As soon as I get home from school I'm going to race over to the paddock and go for a ride.

I'm so lucky – it was the best birthday ever!!!

Tina being a rock star!!! Ha Ha Ha!

Monday 12 November

Just when everything seemed to be going well…

I found a huge cut and a bruise in the shape of a hoof on Sparkle's side. Shelly's horse, Millie has become the boss of the paddock and I'm sure she must have kicked Sparkle. Millie's such a bossy horse and so greedy at feed times. Even though she has food in her own feed bin, she wants Sparkle's as well. She races across the paddock with her ears back and kicks out at Sparkle so she can get her food. Then she races back to her own feed bin to eat that too! She's so greedy! And it's so hard to make sure each horse gets their share when Millie's in the paddock. I think I'm going to have to take Sparkle out and feed her on her own in future.

And now I can't even use my new Wintec because the cut on her side is right in the saddle area. So it'll hurt her too much to have a saddle on. I wonder how long it'll take for the cut to heal? Not too long I hope! I can't believe I won't be able to ride her and just when I have a brand new saddle as well. But Mom said…you get what you focus on! She's always saying that and the strange thing is, she's usually right. So now I'm going to focus on Sparkle getting better quickly so I can use the Wintec and take her for a ride. I bet she'll love the new saddle just as much as me.

I'm going to ask Mom and Dad if I can take the Wintec to school for show and tell – that would be really cool. I'm sure Miss Johnson won't mind. I think I'll ask her tomorrow.

Thursday 15 November

Mom and Dad took me to school today with my new saddle so I could show my class. They really liked it and I had to tell everyone the names of all the parts and how to adjust the stirrups and all. A lot of the kids have never even ridden a horse before so they knew nothing about it. Miss Johnson's such an animal lover, she was really interested as well. She brings her dog to school sometimes. She's a really cute Bassett Hound, called Shelby. Miss Johnson isn't married and doesn't have any kids so Shelby's like her baby. She's such a well-behaved dog and we're allowed to pat her and play with her. She sits right beside Miss Johnson's desk while we're in class – she's so cute! Miss Johnson said that she'll take photos of each of us with Santa hats on holding Shelby and we can use the photos to make Christmas cards.

And also, the BEST news is that Miss Johnson said I can bring Sparkle to school one day next week. Dad said that he would bring her in Tom's trailer and Miss Johnson said he can drive the trailer straight onto the oval. Then we can unload her right there and the whole class can go and look at her. How awesome is that!!! Everyone is so excited! She's such a quiet pony and she loves people, so she'll be fine, I know it. They'll have to keep their distance though. Miss Johnson said we all have to stay safe and no one will be able to get close to her or pat her or anything, but that's okay. It'll just be great to show her to everyone. This is the best thing ever. I bet nobody has ever taken a pony to school for show and tell – not at my school anyway!

I can't wait for next week!

Saturday 17 November

Sparkle's cut has nearly healed but Jim (Cammie and Grace's Dad), said I should wait a few more days before I ride her. It wouldn't be fair to put a saddle on top of that cut – it would hurt her too much and probably make it bleed again, so I just have to wait. It was still fun though because Grace and I were watching the other girls practice their jumping today and we were able to reset the jumps for them when they knocked them down. It was so great watching Kate jump Lulu. Her legs have completely healed and she was flying over the jumps. She can jump over 3 feet – that is so high! I can't wait until I can do that on Sparkle!

Grace and Cammie are still sharing their horse, Rocket and Grace said that because I couldn't ride Sparkle, then she wouldn't ride today either. So we just hung around together in the paddock and had fun. We're becoming such good friends now – we get along really well. She came over and swam in the pool with me this afternoon as well – that was great fun too. I love having a best friend as a neighbor. I'm so lucky.

There are no boys in our street for Nate to play with though, just heaps of girls – and we're all horse mad! He gets annoyed about that and says it isn't fair – but Dad takes him surfing all the time and he goes off motorbike riding with his friends, so he still gets to have fun. Mom says that we're both so lucky to have a property where we can ride horses AND motor bikes.

Nate has tried riding Sparkle and he even had a lesson with Jane, the instructor. But he doesn't like horse riding much. He says that he feels much safer on his motorbike. Mom said it's because he has control of his bike but doesn't feel the same when he's on a horse. I think that motorbikes are scary to ride – not horses! It's okay when he doubles me, but I still get scared. I did try having a go on my own a couple of times and Dad said I just have to practice so I'm more confident. I might try it again – Nate loves it when I ride his bike. But I definitely prefer horses!

We got a great surprise today as well because Tom put some barrels in the paddock so we can practice barrel racing. He brought logs as well and said we can put the logs on the barrels to make more jumps. So now we'll be able to set up a proper jumping course. Ali said we should paint colored stripes on them. I asked Dad and he found some leftover paint in our shed for us to use. He repainted our house last year, so we have heaps of leftover paint and brushes. It was really fun and the barrels and logs look so good – some have blue and white stripes and some have pink and white (the pink was leftover from painting my bedroom).

Ali is really arty. She's so clever and has such great ideas. It was so much fun painting all the equipment together. She also said we should use the spare logs for bounce pony. And we even made some bending poles. Dad found some special thin poles that are perfect and he mixed up cement to put into ice cream containers so we could stand the poles in them.

Now there's so much for us to do rather than just ride around the paddocks. I can't wait to join pony club next year so I can go to gymkhanas and do all of the events. Kate and Shelley have competed in heaps of them and won so many medals and ribbons. I know that Sparkle is a really good sporting pony and she already knows how to do all of these things. As soon as I can ride her again, I'm going to practice on her.

Sunday 18 November

We all met in the paddock again today and set up the jumps. The paint was dry so we could move the barrels and logs around. It looks so cool and now we have our own jumping course. The girls came up with the BEST idea as well. We're going to have our own gymkhana right here in our paddock. We can organize all the events and do jumping, barrels, bounce pony and bending. Ali's going to make some ribbons for the winners and we're going to ask all the parents to come and watch. Kate and Shelley are going to work out a program and get it all typed up so it's really official.

This will be so cool and Mom and Dad think it's a great idea as well. I can't wait!

Shelley with Millie

Tuesday 20 November

Finally, Sparkle's cut has healed and I was able to ride her today. The Wintec is so awesome! It's so comfortable and Sparkle looks perfect with it on her back. It's so much nicer than the shabby old western saddle I was using. Mom says I have to be very grateful that Ali's mom loaned it to me though. And I really am! I think I'll make her a thank you card and take it over to her tomorrow. I think she'll like that.

The Wintec is so much easier to jump in as well. And today I even managed a 2 foot high jump. I'm so proud of myself and of Sparkle too. She's such a good pony and I love watching her ears go forward when she goes over the jumps. I think she loves jumping just as much as me! I have to practice keeping my eyes straight ahead though, facing in the direction that I want her to go. Ali was in the paddock this afternoon helping me – it's so good to have someone telling me what I'm doing wrong. Mom said that I'll learn so much quicker this way. Mom always picks up the jumps if Sparkle knocks any down. She's always in the paddock with me when I ride. She helps me to tack up and tightens the girth when it gets loose. (She'll never forget that again!)

I had the best ride today! After jumping I had a go at barrels, bending and even bounce pony. Sparkle knows exactly what to do. I just have to push her on using my leg aids. She's pretty fast and I'm becoming so much more confident.

I'm going to keep practicing every afternoon if I can, so I'll be ready for our gymkhana. We'll probably have it in a couple of weeks. We have to work out a day when all the girls and the parents are free. Hopefully we'll be able to have it soon.

Oh and the best news as well – Miss Johnson told me today that I can bring Sparkle to school any day this week. I just have to check when Dad can get some time off work to take her. This is so exciting! I can't believe I'll get to take my pony to school for show and tell!

I love jumping!

Thursday 22 November

Oh my gosh!!! Today was incredible. Dad brought Sparkle to school in the horse trailer. It was during the morning session before the morning tea play break. He drove the trailer onto the oval and unloaded her right there. My whole class went down to look at her but Miss Johnson made everyone stand right back, just to be safe.

She asked me to demonstrate how to groom and brush her and how to clean her hooves with the hoof pick. Dad held her lead rope and she just stood there so quietly the whole time. Then Miss Johnson just couldn't resist – she had to go and pat her and she thought she was beautiful. She even gave her a hug.

Then all the kids wanted to pat her too and Miss Johnson said it was okay because she could see how quiet Sparkle is. They all had turns patting her and she just stood there so quietly the whole time. Everyone adored her – she's so well-behaved. Miss Johnson was raving about how beautiful she is and I felt so proud!

Everyone said that it was the best show and tell they've ever seen. And so did Miss Johnson. I'm so lucky to have her for a teacher. And I'm so lucky to have Sparkle for a pony.

Tuesday 11 December

I can't believe it's been almost 3 whole weeks since I've had a chance to write! I never seem to get much time for my diary lately - things have been so hectic lately, especially with all the horses.

Grace now has her own pony – a beautiful 14 hand chestnut called, Trixie. So now she won't have to share Rocket with Cammie. They'll each have their own pony and this is perfect for our gymkhana. We've decided to have it on the Saturday after Christmas because everyone's busy until then.

I can't believe that Christmas is only 14 days away and the school holidays are almost here! In 3 days I'll have 6 weeks off school and I'll be able to spend every day with Sparkle. The girls and I are so excited. We have so much planned! We're going to have sleep-overs at each other's houses and go riding EVERY day. We'll have to get up really early to ride though because it's SO hot now. Yesterday was almost 100 degrees and way too hot for riding! But the early mornings are perfect and so are the late afternoons when it cools down. I think that's my favorite time. It's so good in summer because it gets dark so much later and we now have more time in the afternoons to ride.

I'm so glad we have a pool! It's so hot, we'll be able to go swimming every day. And Grace and Cammie are getting a pool put in too. They're hoping it'll be ready for Christmas.

And the best news is, they're now going to keep their two horses in our front paddock rather than at Ali's. Our front paddock is right across the road from their driveway and it's much quicker and easier for them to feed and look after their horses. So Dad is going to buy a heap of special wire and posts to fence the paddock for them. The money that Jim pays Dad for keeping Rocket and Trixie will help to pay for Sparkle. We've started giving her special food and it's really expensive. But she seems to be getting skinny and we don't know why. We're hoping that the new food will fatten her up and make her really healthy. I'm so happy because the girls will be at my house all the time now, instead of always being at Ali's. This is going to be so cool!

I can't wait for Christmas. My list this year is full of horsey stuff. I might even get those jodhpurs that I've been wanting. They're so expensive, I still haven't saved up enough to buy them myself. Luckily Ali has given me her old ones to wear and Mom even found some blue ones at the 2nd hand shop that almost look brand new. And they fit me perfectly! I'd love to have the brand new pair that I saw at Saddle World though. I know they still have them because I saw them when I was in there with Grace the other day. Maybe Santa will give them to me?

I can't wait!

Grace's new pony, Trixie. So pretty!

Tuesday 25 Dec

We had an awesome Christmas Day!

Nate and I got up at 5am and ran in to wake up Mom and Dad. But we had to wait for Nana to get up and make a cup of tea before we could start opening our presents. She always takes so long! She arrived a few days ago and she's staying for 2 weeks. I was really excited because I thought that she could come to the gymkhana, but Mom said that she probably won't be able to make it across our creek. She's pretty wobbly when she walks and needs some help. Mom said that she'll have to get her a special walker soon so that she can get around easily.

I got the best presents and Santa gave me the jodhpurs I wanted. They're exactly the same as the ones in Saddle World and they look so cool. I tried them on and they fit perfectly. I'm so glad that he got the size right!

I got a new pair of chaps as well – they're the same as Ali's. I've been wanting some like hers for ages. As well as that I got some new riding boots. Now I don't have to wear Ali's hand me downs - but Mom said that I should still keep them as a spare pair. It's always good to have a pair to lend to friends when they come over for a ride, so they'll be perfect for that.

I got a brand new grooming kit as well. Sparkle stepped on my old one and the case is all broken, so now I'll have lots of brushes. When my friends come over there'll be plenty of brushes to groom Sparkle with. I also got a new purple lead rope. I've just been using a faded old green one that Josh's mom gave me when we brought Sparkle home. This one will look so much better!

I LOVE SPARKLE!!

It's funny because I got pretty much all horsey stuff and Nate got things for motorbike riding. He also got a drum kit. Mom says that he's spoilt but Dad says that it's fair because I have Sparkle. Dad wants us all to be musicians and play instruments like him. Nate is really good on the guitar and I guess now, he'll have to learn the drums as well. He's so excited about it. At least he can play them in Dad's music room up at our shed. Lucky it's sound proof!

I made Sparkle a special mash for her Christmas breakfast. I chopped up apples and carrots and added her favorite – some mashed banana. Then I mixed it with oats and chaff and added some of her favorite grass hay. She thought it was delicious! You should have seen her licking her lips. It was so cute! She kept dropping bits on the ground but that made Sheba happy. I think she enjoyed it as much as Sparkle! Sheba's our golden retriever and she ÁLWAYS comes over to the paddock with me when I go to ride or feed Sparkle. She loves it and always has her nose in a bush somewhere. All we can see is her backside and tail poking out and her tail is always wagging. She's so happy just sniffing around looking to see what she can find. She's great in the paddock too and loves wandering around when I'm riding. The horses are used to her and don't mind her at all.

It's so funny because my cat Soxy - who is the most adorable ginger cat you've ever seen - has started coming over to the paddock with us. Mom says it looks hilarious. There's me, Sheba and Soxy all walking together. I would have thought a cat would be scared of horses but Soxy loves it over there. When we get to the creek though, I have to carry him. He just sits there looking at me and waiting to be picked up. The creek is really low at the moment because we haven't had rain for ages. So he can jump across without getting wet. When there's more water in it though, I have to carefully cross by jumping from one big rock to another. Dad's going to get a proper crossing made soon. That'll be so much better. He's just worried about it getting washed away if the creek floods. This happens when there's lots of rain, but hopefully he'll be able to work something out.

I had the best Christmas! Mom, Dad, Nate and Nana loved the presents I gave them as well. It was great this year because I saved enough money from feeding all the horses and I could buy really good presents for everyone.

Now we've got the gymkhana to look forward to! We're going to have it next Saturday afternoon and that's actually New Year's Eve. The girls are all really excited and so am I!

I LOVE CHRISTMAS!

Tuesday 1 January

New Year's Day!

Yesterday we finally got to have our gymkhana. We spent all morning getting ready and we were so excited! The girls and I set up a really cool jumping course, the bending poles and also bounce pony. The paddock looked so good with all the colored stripes that we painted on the equipment. And we were so glad that the weather was fine! We were really worried because there's a cyclone up north and the weatherman said that heavy rain and flooding is on the way. But there was no sign of it at our place, just more beaming sunshine.

The parents started arriving at 3:00 in the afternoon. They all brought fold up chairs and we set them up under the shade of some trees. So they had a really good spot to sit. Dad even drove Nana around to Ali's place and set up a comfy chair for her in the shade so she could watch the gymkhana from there. They all brought some drinks and snacks and said they were getting ready to celebrate New Year's Eve.

It all started off really well. We each did the jumping course a couple of times. In the end we decided not to score each other, but just have fun. Tom was helping us all with our jumping and pretty much giving us each a jumping lesson as we went along. This was really cool because he knows a lot about jumping and was really helpful. Then everyone ended up getting a ribbon. Ali ended up making one for everyone!

Just as we were about to start the other events, we suddenly heard a scream. Cammie decided to take Rocket for a ride in the big paddock and for some reason, he bolted. Then almost in a flash I saw Cammie on the ground. She had fallen off Rocket and then he raced off up the hill. Everyone went running towards her in a panic – it was really scary!

I felt my heart stop and I couldn't move. I could see her lying on the ground but she was completely still. Her Dad bent over her and we just stood waiting – I was really hoping that she was okay. Then he moved away from her and she slowly stood up. She was shaken up and she was crying. I was praying that she wasn't hurt. We've heard terrible stories of people coming off horses and being badly injured and I didn't want that happening to Cammie.

She took her helmet off and sat down with all the parents. Tom then went to catch Rocket and we all rushed over to her – we were so worried, but thank goodness, she was fine. She told us to go on with the gymkhana, so we did but it kind of wasn't the same after that.

Then Shelley and Kate's parents said that they had to go and get ready for New Year's Eve. Cammie, Grace and Ali asked me if they could stay the night at my house. Their parents said that they might come over as well and have a barbecue with us. Mom and Dad said that this was a great idea.

The girls and I decided to set the tent up so we could camp out for the night, just like at my birthday party. So Dad helped us get organized and set up while Mom got the food ready. Thank goodness, Cammie wasn't hurt badly. She said that her wrist hurt a bit from the fall and she had some bruises on her hip, but that was all. She was so lucky!

I ended up having so much fun with the girls last night and Nate joined in as well. We had a nighttime swim in the pool and later on we all got torches and played spotlight. It gets so dark on our property at nighttime though and hiding in the bushes can get pretty scary. There was a lot of screaming going on, that's for sure! Then Mom and Dad gave us some sparklers and party poppers and we let them off right on midnight. We all counted down and then called out HAPPY NEW YEAR!!!!!

Finally we went to sleep in the tent. Mom and Dad had to get up during the night though because it started to rain and they wanted to check that we weren't getting wet. Then at about 6:00 this morning, Jim arrived to pick the girls up. That was so early for them to leave and the bad part was, I was left to clean up all the mess!

Now it's pouring with rain. Mom and Dad said that it's meant to get worse and there might even be flooding. I hope my baby is okay. I brought her down near the house this afternoon so she could graze on the nice grass. But there's thunder and lightning right now so I hope she's not getting spooked! I wish I had stables to keep her in, so she can stay nice and dry. I'm glad she now has a summer rug! That will help to protect her from some of the rain at least.

Oh no – the lights are flickering. This storm definitely seems to be getting worse. I hope we don't have a blackout! I don't think I'm going to be able to sleep tonight – I'm too worried about Sparkle! Maybe I should go and look for her and check that she's safe. I can't stop thinking about her. Is she going to be alright????

The rain won't stop! The creek is flooding!

I'm worried about Sparkle!!!

Find out what happens to Sparkle

in Book 2 of

Diary of a Horse Mad Girl...

Thank you for reading my book.

If you enjoyed it, I would be very grateful if you would leave a review on Amazon.

Your support really does make a difference!

Please Like our Diary of a Horse Mad Girl Facebook page

- A fabulous page for all horse loving girls…

https://www.facebook.com/DiaryofaHorseMadGirl

And be sure to follow us on Instagram

@juliajonesdiary

Have you read the Julia Jones' Diary series yet...

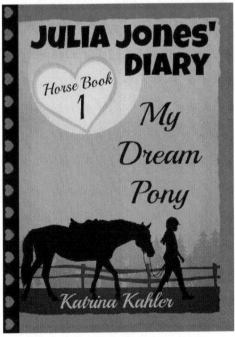

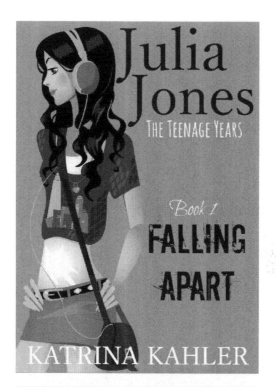

Here are some more books that you are sure to enjoy…

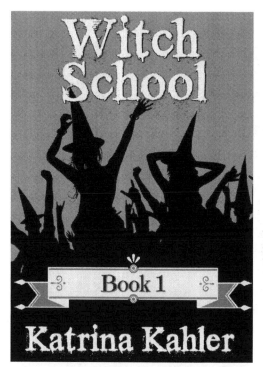

HOW TO MAKE
FRIENDS
AND BE POPULAR

GIRLS ONLY!

KATRINA KAHLER
KAZ CAMPBELL

PUBERTY
PERIODS
AND ALL THAT STUFF!

GIRLS ONLY!

KATRINA KAHLER
KAZ CAMPBELL

Made in the USA
Lexington, KY
19 March 2017